SACR/

Sa

D0209247

LIN OLIVER

THE FANTASTIC FRAME

For Trudi, and that fun day in the Tate Modern—LO

To Amanda, who helped me write this dedication—SK

GROSSET & DUNLAP
Penguin Young Readers Group
An Imprint of Penguin Random House LLC

Penguin supports copyright. Copyright fuels creativity, encourages diverse
voices, promotes free speech, and creates a vibrant culture. Thank you for
buying an authorized edition of this book and for complying with copyright laws
by not reproducing, scanning, or distributing any part of it in any form without
permission. You are supporting writers and allowing Penguin to continue to
publish books for every reader.

The publisher does not have any control over and does not assume any responsibility
for author or third-party websites or their content.

Text copyright © 2016 by Lin Oliver. Illustrations copyright © 2016 by Samantha Kallis.
All rights reserved. Published by Grosset & Dunlap, an imprint of Penguin Random
House LLC, 345 Hudson Street, New York, New York 10014. GROSSET & DUNLAP is a
trademark of Penguin Random House LLC. Manufactured in China.

Library of Congress Cataloging-in-Publication Data is available.

ISBN 978-0-448-48087-9 | 10 9 8 7 6 5 4 3 2 1

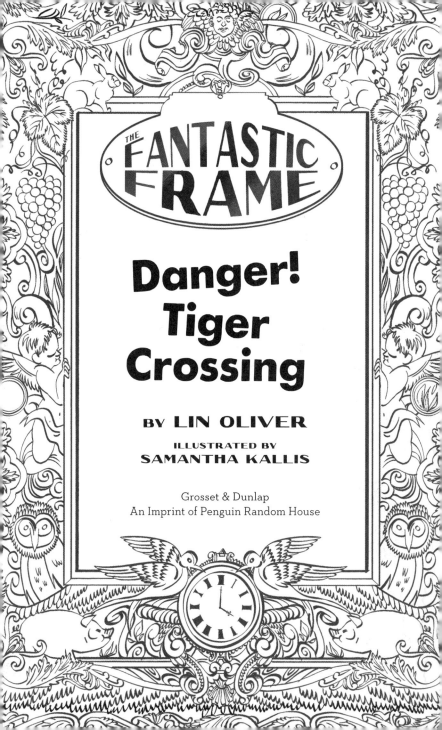

THE FANTASTIC FRAME

Danger! Tiger Crossing

BY **LIN OLIVER**

ILLUSTRATED BY
SAMANTHA KALLIS

Grosset & Dunlap
An Imprint of Penguin Random House

CHAPTER 1

"I saw a giant orange pig on our swing set this morning," said my little sister, Maggie. "He was wearing a fancy black hat."

We were eating tuna melts at the kitchen table in our new house.

"Of course he was," I said. "And I bet he was playing 'Jingle Bells' on the tuba."

"Everyone knows pigs don't play the tuba," Maggie snapped, sticking her tongue out at me.

I decided not to continue this conversation. Four-year-olds say weird things, and there's no point trying to talk sense into them. The other day, it took me an hour to convince Maggie that bananas don't dance. But our mom, being our mom, felt the little bubble brain deserved a serious answer.

"It would be very unusual to see an orange pig on our swing set, honey," my mom said, wiping a long string of gooey cheese off Maggie's chin.

"At least one with a fancy hat," my dad added.

Maggie slammed her sandwich down on her plate. She can have a bad temper when she wants to.

"I saw him." She pouted. "He also had

on a white shirt buttoned all the way up
his blobby pig neck and a red bow tie with
polka dots."

"This is ridiculous," I told her. "There's
no way a pig could tie a tie. I don't even
know how to do it, and I'm a ten-year-old
human. You're just making up this whole
story to get attention."

"Tiger Brooks!" My mom frowned at me.
"Don't be so harsh with your sister, young
man. She just has a very active imagination.
Now clear the table, please."

*Wait a minute! Maggie talks like a crazy
person and I get in trouble?*

Who made that rule?

At least clearing the table got me out
of doing the Saturday deliveries with my
mom. She had twenty cakes to deliver that

afternoon. Her business is called Cakes by Cookie, which sounds stupid until you realize that her name is Cookie. She bakes fancy cakes, mostly for little kids' birthday parties. She's been doing really well, which is how our family got the extra money to move into a bigger place from our small apartment in our old neighborhood. I had no interest in spending my first Saturday in our new house dropping off Elmo cakes.

Lucky for me, Maggie wanted to go with Mom. Dad announced that he was going to take a nap, so I did the dishes and cleaned up. Afterward, I checked my new Batman watch, the one my uncle Cole gave me when I told him I couldn't tell time the old-fashioned way. It took me a while to learn, but now I could read the hands. It was only three o'clock. That left me the rest of the afternoon to set up my lab, with no four-year-olds telling me their imaginary pig stories.

My lab is what other people would call my bedroom. I like to call it a lab because it's where science takes place. Science Tiger Brooks-style, that is. I take things apart to see how they work: clocks, radios, old tricycles, robots, windup dinosaurs—whatever I can find. Then I try to put them back together. Sometimes I do it right. But mostly, I make weird things like a toaster with wheels, or a dinosaur that ticks, or a kitchen chair that roars.

I had a lot of unpacking to do. The first box, which was labeled "HANDS OFF AND THAT MEANS YOU, MAGGIE" was filled

with nuts, bolts, cogs, gears, and screws. The next carton had about a million remote controls I had collected that had gotten separated from their machines.

As I picked up that box, one of the remotes fell out and got jammed between my bed and the wall. Suddenly, I heard a whirring sound. Looking around, I saw that my radio-controlled helicopter had taken off. It circled my room and sailed out the window into the backyard.

I grabbed the remote and ran into the living room. My dad was on the couch, snoring like a grizzly bear. I dashed past him into the backyard, just in time to see my helicopter cruise by the swing set and disappear over the neighbor's fence.

"Hey, get back here!" I called out. I tried

using the controller, but the helicopter was out of range.

As I ran toward the fence, I noticed a weird pattern in the grass under the swing set. It looked like footprints, except they weren't human footprints. Each print was divided into two sections and was pointed at the top. Could they be hoofprints? They didn't look like horse hoofprints.

Wait a minute! Pigs have hooves.

Stop it, Tiger, I said to myself. *You are not four years old. You do not see imaginary pigs. Just find your helicopter and go back into the lab.*

I dragged one of the lawn chairs over to the fence. I hopped up and looked into the neighbor's yard.

The grass in the yard was as tall as

Maggie. No one had mowed it in years. There was a barbecue covered with rust and spiderwebs. A long clothesline with sheets hanging on it stretched across the whole yard. The sheets were splattered with paint—big splotches of red and purple and yellow and orange. Behind one of those sheets, I could just make out—no, even I didn't believe it!

I stared hard and long. Then I *had* to believe it. My eyes don't lie. It was a black top hat poking out from behind the sheets.

"I see you," I said to the hat.

There was no answer.

"Whoever you are, if you have my helicopter, give it back."

Something moved behind the sheets. I looked down and saw hooves attached to what looked like puffy orange legs!

Suddenly, a strong breeze came up and blew the sheet off the line. Standing in front of me was a large orange pig wearing a black top hat, a white shirt, and a red polka-dot bow tie. He was holding my helicopter.

"It's you," I whispered. "The one Maggie saw."

A woman's voice, old and shrill, came
from inside the house.

"Chives," the voice called. "Come in here
right now. I need more blue!"

The pig gave me what I think was a smile
and tipped his top hat.

"I'm very pleased to meet you, good sir,"
he said.

I was so shocked, I couldn't move. I just

stared at him with my mouth hanging open.

"Chives!" the woman called again. "Right now!"

"If you'll excuse me, Madame is calling," he said.

Clutching my helicopter, the pig hurried through the back door of the house. I stood there, still as a statue.

Then I felt a cold, sticky hand on my shoulder. I spun around so fast, I fell off the lawn chair and landed facedown on the grass. I was afraid to look up, afraid of what I might see. The ice-cold hand of a ghost? A zombie with no face? If a talking orange pig lived next door, maybe something even weirder was lurking in my own backyard.

CHAPTER 2

I stayed perfectly still with my face planted in the grass. I hoped that whatever it was would just go away. But it didn't.

"You can look up now," a voice said. "I'm not that scary." I uncovered my eyes and saw a girl about my own age. That was a relief! She had long black hair and was wearing a crazy-looking hat made out of bird feathers.

"I'm Luna," she said. "That means *moon* in Spanish."

"I'm Tiger," I answered. "That means *tiger* in English."

"You're funny," she said with a laugh. "Do you like my hat? I made it myself."

"It's very . . . um . . . feathery," I said, pulling myself to my feet. "After you finished it, there must have been a lot of bald birds around here."

She laughed again.

"I collect feathers and lots of other things, too. Buttons and seashells and shiny pennies. I keep all my stuff in my magic cave. You can come see it, if you want."

"You have your own cave?"

"Sort of," Luna said. "It's really my

bedroom. We live upstairs from you. That's my window, the one with the purple curtains. I think purple is the coolest color, don't you?"

My mom had mentioned that a family named Lopez lived in the apartment upstairs. But she'd never said anything about a Bird Girl. A Bird Girl who was also a major blabberhead.

"I can tell you all about our street," Luna was saying. "Like, the ice-cream truck comes Saturdays at two o'clock. You just missed it. I like lime Popsicles best. I just had one, but it melted in my hand before I could finish it."

That explained the cold, sticky hand. But it didn't explain the talking orange pig. I had to know more.

"Luna," I began very carefully. "Do you ever see any strange creatures around here?"

"Sure. The other day I found a really hairy caterpillar eating an avocado that fell off the tree. It's pretty strange that caterpillars like guacamole, don't you think? And Mrs. Hoskins across the street has a parrot named Smarty Pants who can say the alphabet all the way up to Q."

"Anything even weirder than that?" I asked. "Anything . . . like . . . let's say . . . in the pig family?"

Luna looked very surprised. She got close to me, so close that some of her feathers brushed my face.

"You mean you saw it?" she whispered. "The talking orange pig?"

I nodded. "His name is Chives."

"He's never told me his name," she said. "I've only seen him a few times. When he sees me, he runs back into the house."

"He lives there? Next door to us?"

"Yes, with Viola Dots. She's really old and has lived in that house for, like, fifty years. Nobody on the street has ever seen her. She never comes outside."

"Not ever?"

Luna shook her head. "Once a week, someone from the store comes to deliver groceries. They ring the doorbell and leave them on the front porch. My mom says I have to stay away from there."

"Did you tell your mom about the orange pig?" I asked her.

"I told my grandma. She watches me

during the day when my mom is at school."

"And did your grandma call the police? Or the zoo? Or the Weird Animal Patrol?"

"No. She's from Mexico, and her English isn't very good."

"But somebody has to report this," I said. "We can't just let talking pigs run loose in the neighborhood."

"He doesn't run loose," Luna said. "He stays inside. My grandmother says that you shouldn't bother things that don't bother you. So I've never told anyone else."

I started to pace back and forth on the grass. My head was spinning with everything I had seen and heard. Part of me felt scared. It's creepy to move into a house next to a talking pig and a crazy old lady who no one has seen in fifty years. But part of me also felt curious. The same kind of curious I get when I take something apart to see how it works. I just have to know the answer.

"Luna," I said. "Do you think we could get a look inside the house?"

"I've tried," she said. "All the windows are covered with thick curtains. You can't see a thing."

"What about the front door?" I asked.

"I told you. They don't answer the doorbell."

"Have you ever tried?"

"No."

"Well, I'm going to," I said.

"Tiger, they won't open the door. And even if they do, you have no idea what you'll find inside there. People say Viola Dots is mean and crazy."

"Thanks for the warning, Luna. I'll let you know what I find."

I ran along the side of the house until I came to the sidewalk. I hid behind some bushes and studied Viola Dots's house. It must have been blue at one time, but most of the paint had chipped off. The front door was covered with spiderwebs. At the top of the house was a round tower with a little window. I stared up at it. Was that an eye I saw looking back at me?

My heart beat a little faster. The eye disappeared.

And then I felt it again, a cold hand on my shoulder. This time, I knew who it was. It smelled like limes.

"I'm coming with you," Luna whispered in my ear.

Together we crouched down low and crept to the front of the house. Slowly, I pushed open the creaky gate. Then we headed up the path that was overgrown with weeds.

When we reached the front door, I turned to Luna.

"This is your last chance to leave," I warned her.

"I'm in if you're in," she answered.

With a shaky hand, I reached up and rang the doorbell.

CHAPTER 3

No one answered. So I rang the bell again. Still nothing.

"I told you, no one comes to the door," Luna said. "Let's just go."

"Wait. I'm going to try one more thing."

Lifting up the rusty old door knocker that was shaped like a paintbrush, I pounded on the door five or six times.

"Hello in there!" I called out. "I've come for my helicopter."

I thought I heard something moving inside, footsteps scurrying around. I guess I should say hoofsteps, because I had a feeling that's what they were. The door opened just a crack, enough for me to see an orange pig snout sticking out.

"Apologies," Chives said. "I didn't mean to run off with your toy, but the mistress can be an impatient woman."

"You mean Viola Dots?" Luna said. "We'd love to meet her."

"I'm afraid that will be impossible," he answered.

"Mrs. Dots does not receive visitors.

However, if you wait here, I will get your helicopter, which I have placed upstairs for safekeeping."

The snout disappeared, leaving the door slightly open.

"Are you thinking what I think you're thinking?" Luna asked. "Because if you are, I wouldn't do it."

"That's the difference between you and me," I answered.

I pushed on the door and it swung open.

"Come on," I said. "Let's just take a quick look around. We'll be back on the porch by the time Chives comes back downstairs."

I had assumed that the living room would be dark and dusty, full of creepy old furniture. But it was just the opposite. The inside was one huge room. There was

no furniture at all. Lots of dangling crystal lights hung down from the ceiling.

"Wow," Luna whispered. "It's all twinkly in here, like a fairy-tale castle."

Big paintings of every kind leaned against the walls. One showed tall stacks of golden hay. Another was of a wild-looking starry night, with crazy splotches of blue and yellow. There was even one of a naked lady standing in what looked like a giant clamshell.

On the biggest wall hung a huge golden frame. It was old and dusty, carved with rabbits and owls and pigs and angels. All the creatures were connected by leafy trees and bunches of grapes. On the bottom of the frame, there was the fanciest clock I'd ever seen. It was made of gold, just like the

two birds that were surrounding it. The
clock didn't seem to work, though. The
hands said five o'clock. I checked my watch.
It was ten to four. Batman is never wrong.

Inside the golden frame was a painting
that sent a shiver down my spine. There
was something about it that seemed so
frightening, like being in the middle of

a bad dream. It was a picture of a tiger crouched in a thick green jungle. His yellow eyes were wide and glowing. His sharp teeth looked like they were dying for something to bite. It felt like that tiger was going to jump out of the frame and pounce on me at any second.

"What exactly is the meaning of this?"

I knew that voice, old and shrill, could only belong to Viola Dots.

She burst into the room and marched up to us, her face set in a deep frown. She was wearing a beaded headband, a peace symbol necklace, and a large, paint-splattered shirt. When she pointed at me, I noticed her wrinkled hands were covered in paint, too.

"I don't believe you were invited in," she said.

"I just came to get
my helicopter," I tried to
explain.

"Chives!" she
hollered. "Bring the child
his toy."

Chives came clopping
down the wooden stairs and handed me my
helicopter. He had put it on a silver tray.

"There," Viola Dots said. "You have it.
Now leave."

This woman was not someone I wanted
to argue with. She scared me. It looked like
she hadn't smiled in fifty years.

"On my way, ma'am," I said. "By the way,
that's a fantastic frame you have there."

"Indeed it is," she said. "Now as I was
saying, good-bye."

I turned to leave. To my surprise, Luna stayed back. That girl would talk to anyone.

"Did you do all these paintings?" Luna asked Viola.

Viola Dots nodded her head, which made her dangling jeweled earrings sparkle like the crystal lights on the ceiling.

"You're a very good painter, Mrs. Dots," Luna said. "I paint, too, in my magic cave."

"Don't talk nonsense, child," Viola Dots answered.

"I like what you're wearing," Luna went on in her friendly, chatty way. "Your headband is cool. And I especially love your earrings. I collect glittery stuff, too, just like you."

Viola didn't answer, but that didn't seem to bother Luna one bit. She chatted right on.

"And I make a lot of beautiful things, like capes and jewelry and costumes." Luna was talking a mile a minute now. "See this feather hat I made? Want to see it close up?"

Before Viola could say no, Luna walked right up to her.

"I collected these feathers from all over the neighborhood, except some of them my grandma bought at a thrift store. And then I arranged them to look like a bird I saw in my dreams."

Viola listened impatiently, not smiling, but not exactly frowning either. I looked over at Chives. He was definitely smiling, at least as much as pigs can smile.

"Your creations are indeed lovely, young miss," he said to Luna.

I still couldn't believe those words were coming from a talking pig.

"Some of the kids at school make fun of what I wear," Luna said. "But I don't care. I like to be original."

"Yes," Viola Dots said, taking a step toward one of her paintings. "All art requires originality."

"Maybe you can come over to my house sometime," Luna said to Viola. "You like to make art, and so do I. I can show you all my supplies."

Viola looked surprised.

"Come to your house?" she repeated. "That's impossible."

"Madame Dots does not leave the house," Chives explained. "She hasn't been outside in over fifty years now. Not since the day her son, David, disappeared."

"Disappeared? What happened to him?" The question flew out of my mouth before I could stop it.

"I don't speak of that day," Viola said. "Never! Now go, and let me be."

I headed for the door. Luna followed me for a few steps. But then she turned and went back to Viola. She reached out and took Viola's paint-splattered hands. Viola seemed shocked, but she didn't pull her hands away.

"My grandma says that everything feels worse when you keep it inside," Luna said.

"Perhaps the child is right, Madame," Chives said. "Perhaps it's time we spoke of it."

Viola Dots shook her head.

"There are so many memories," she said. "So many questions. And so few answers."

She went over to the frame and ran her hand along the carvings. She reached up and touched the tiger, following its stripes with her finger.

"I remember that awful day as if it were yesterday," she said.

Then Viola Dots took out a handkerchief, dabbed at her eyes, and started to speak.

CHAPTER 4

"It happened on the day my husband and I brought this frame home," Viola Dots began. "We had purchased it from an antiques store. The shop owner said the frame was magical. He kept talking nonsense about what he called its 'hour of power.' Of course, we just laughed at that. We hung the frame on the wall and placed one of my paintings inside."

"The tiger one?" Luna asked.

"No. The tiger painting is my latest. I have done hundreds of paintings in my life. I have painted copies of the great masterpieces of art." She pointed to the paintings around the room.

"Wait. So you didn't think up this painting yourself?" I asked.

"Of course not," Viola said. "This is a copy of a very well-known painting by Henri Rousseau. Certainly you've heard of him."

Actually, I hadn't. Boy, did I feel stupid. But Chives came to my rescue.

"Sir, Rousseau's original painting is called *Surprised!*" he whispered in my ear. "It hangs in the National Gallery of London. It is quite famous in art circles."

"Sorry," I whispered back. "I'm not much of an art guy."

Viola continued with her story.

"The painting Charles and I put in the frame that day was one of my originals," she explained. "It showed a violent storm over a remote castle in England. I called it *Trouble in the Kingdom*."

"That's a cool title," Luna said, nodding.

"Our son, David, was thirteen at the time," Viola went on.

"That afternoon, David was practicing the piano over there, near the frame. Suddenly, I heard a ripping sound, like the canvas was tearing in two."

"The painting just ripped apart for no reason?" Luna asked.

"A hole the size of a fist opened up in the painting," Viola said. "The sound of thunder and pounding rain poured out of it. I saw David being pulled toward the hole. Then there was a bolt of lightning, and suddenly David disappeared inside the painting. Just like that, he was swallowed up, leaving no trace behind."

"You mean the painting ate him?" I asked.

"We don't know exactly how any of it happened," Chives said. "Only that young David vanished into the hole in the painting.

In return, I was spit out. I've been living here in this house with Mrs. Dots ever since."

"You were once in a painting?" Luna asked. "So that's why you're that awesome shade of orange."

"My painting was called *Orange Pig with Tie*," Chives said proudly. "It hung in the great hall at Foxley Castle next to a portrait of a hunting dog with a rabbit in its mouth. It hung there for hundreds of years until one day, a violent storm hit the castle."

"Oh," I whispered, almost to myself. "Trouble in the kingdom."

"You have a clever mind, young sir," Chives said. "The next thing I knew, the windows in the great hall had blown open, and a boy of thirteen flew in on a tremendous gust of wind."

"Was it David?" Luna asked.

"It must have been. I reached for him, but the wind was so strong it knocked my painting off the wall. I felt myself tumbling round and round, falling through a dark tunnel. I saw an opening at the end, a light with a hand reaching through it. I sped toward it."

"And then you popped out here, in Mrs. Dots's living room," Luna said.

Chives nodded.

"The hole in the painting closed up," he added softly, "leaving me with no way to go home."

He was quiet for a moment. Then he stood up straight, adjusted his bow tie, and put on a cheerful smile. "But we have made the best of it, haven't we, Madame?"

Mrs. Dots just shook her head.

"For over fifty years now," she said with a sigh, "David has been gone. And I am left with a pig for a butler."

She dabbed at her eyes again. She didn't look quite so mean anymore—just sad.

"You must miss your son very much," Luna said.

"My husband has spent every day since then traveling the world," she said. "He has searched everywhere for David. And I have devoted these years to painting copies of the great masterworks of art. Each new painting goes into that frame. Each time, I hope that David will appear in one of them, that he will come back."

"Wow," Luna said. "He'd be pretty old by now."

"The world of art is timeless," Viola said. "The people we see in paintings live on forever, unchanged."

While Viola and Luna talked, I wandered over to the frame to have a closer look. There had to be some way to figure out what had happened to David. If there's one thing I know about science, even Tiger Brooks–style science, it's that there's a reason for everything. Paintings don't just gobble people up without some explanation.

Handing my helicopter to Chives, I knelt down in front of the clock. I noticed that the little hand, the one on the number five, was bent out of shape. I adjusted it until it was perfectly straight. That was enough to get it to move. I twirled it around so the clock now said four o'clock. I checked my Batman watch. Yup, it was four o'clock.

"All fixed," I said to Chives.

"Well done, sir," he answered, handing me back my helicopter.

As soon as I took my hand off the clock, a loud boom of thunder echoed throughout the living room. It was immediately followed by the whistling of wind and then the plunking of heavy raindrops. Where were those sounds coming from? Definitely not from outside.

I looked across the room and saw Mrs. Dots staring at the painting. Her mouth was open and her eyes looked wild.

"It can't be!" she screamed.

But it was. I put my ear up to the painting. The storm was coming from inside.

Then I heard the rip, like paper being torn in two pieces. A small hole opened up in the painting, right next to where the tiger was crouching.

"The hole!" I yelled, my voice full of panic. "I can see it!"

"Tiger!" Luna called. "What's going on?"

In no time, the hole had become as large as my fist. The storm was raging now, the wind blowing fiercely. It swept me off my feet and pulled me closer and closer to the hole in the painting.

"Help!" I shouted. "Someone please help me!"

"Grab on to something," Viola cried. "Hold on tight!"

She started across the room, but she was old and moved slowly. Chives was nearby and reached one of his stubby arms out to help me. His hoof was pointy and sharp, and I couldn't hold on.

By then, Luna was at my side. Still clutching my helicopter in one hand, too afraid to let go, I held out my other hand to her.

"Pull me back!" I called to her. "I'm scared."

"Me too!" she cried.

She grabbed my hand and tugged as hard as she could. The power of the storm was too much for even the two of us. Screaming at the top of our lungs, we were sucked into the hole in the painting.

"I'm coming with you," I could hear Viola Dots yell.

"No, Madame," I heard Chives answer. "You will not survive."

As the living room disappeared before our eyes, the last thing we saw was Viola's hand reaching through the painting.

I could hear her crying, "David! My David! Come home!"

And then I could no longer hear her or any sounds from the real world. Luna and I were tumbling down a long flight of stairs into a darkness far below. The wind roared and the rain pounded.

Somewhere in the distance, I thought I heard a tiger roar.

CHAPTER 5

We landed with a thud. Darkness was all around. Above me, I saw thousands of stairs, climbing steeply up to nowhere. In front of me, I could barely make out what looked like dark blue-black leaves. The ground felt soggy and wet beneath me.

"Tiger, where are we?" Luna asked.

"I'm not sure," I answered. "But there's only one way to find out."

I tucked my helicopter into the pocket

of my shorts so I could put both arms out
in front of me. The air was hot. Heavy silver
raindrops fell all around us. As we took
a few steps forward, the light grew bright
enough for us to see that we were in the
middle of a jungle. Tall trees with vines
wrapped around their trunks surrounded us
on all sides.

"It's the jungle in the painting," Luna said. "It's exactly the same."

"Do you think we're *actually* inside it?" I asked.

Luna didn't answer. She just shivered with fear. That said it all.

"See those red flowers over there?" she said. "They were in the painting, next to the tiger."

The tiger! If we were truly in the painting, there would be a tiger. Where was he?

A sudden bolt of lightning flashed across the sky and lit up the face of the tiger. He was crouched behind a group of ferns, at exactly the same spot where he was in the painting. His yellow eyes were glowing. His mouth was open. He looked hungry.

"Is he real?" Luna said.

The tiger sniffed the air. His yellow eyes followed even my slightest movement.

"Oh yeah, he's real, all right," I whispered. "We need to get out of here now."

I grabbed Luna's hand, and we took off running. The jungle was thick with trees and vines, ferns and flowers. The wind blew the rain into our faces. I had no idea where we were going. I glanced behind. The tiger was following us across the jungle floor, breathing hard and showing his sharp teeth!

One thing I know for sure . . . you can't outrun a tiger. They can run up to thirty-five miles per hour. If we were going to escape him, we had to think of something else. Luna knew that, too.

"Over there," she called out, pointing to a tall tree. "Let's climb to the top."

"No good," I panted. I could barely talk because I was running so fast. "Tigers are cats. They climb trees."

Up ahead we saw a patch of waist-high thick grass. We ducked behind it to catch our breath. It was quiet for the moment. There was no sound except the plop of the raindrops hitting the soggy ground.

"I think he's gone," Luna whispered, peering out from behind the tangle of tall grasses. "Maybe we lost him."

A large striped paw suddenly shot through the thicket. Its long claws swiped at the air right next to our faces.

"No!" I screamed.

Without a word, Luna grabbed my hand and we bolted out of the grass, deeper into the dark jungle. I didn't dare to look behind me. I knew the tiger was there. He was so close I could hear him breathing. I didn't want to imagine his big black nostrils going in and out with each breath.

"Look! A river!" Luna cried. "I can see it beyond those trees."

"We can make it there. Just put your head down and run."

"Don't worry about me," she called. "I can run like the wind."

And she did, her feathered hat flying in the air.

The tiger was still close behind when we reached the banks of the river. Luna and I jumped into the water without a second thought. There could have been a million crocodiles in there, but we didn't care. We just wanted to escape the jaws of that tiger.

When he saw us in the river, the tiger let out an angry roar. I started to shake—not from the cold, but just from being scared.

"It's okay," Luna whispered to me. "We're safe. At least for now."

Not true. The tiger waded into the river and started paddling his way toward us.

"I didn't know they could swim," I cried. "What do we do now?"

"Swim faster!" a voice called out.

"I could have thought of that," I said to Luna.

"Thought of what? I didn't say anything."

"You didn't just tell me to swim faster?"

"Nope."

I looked around to see whose voice I had heard, but I didn't see anyone. Was that voice coming from high in the treetops? Or was it coming from under the water? Or was I imagining it? I couldn't tell.

"Find the cave," the voice said. I turned

to Luna to see if she had heard it, too, but she was already swimming toward the other side. I put my head into the water and took off after her. With that tiger closing in on us, we had no choice. We had to swim for our lives.

CHAPTER 6

Luna and I never stopped to take a breath. We swam frantically toward the opposite bank. When we got to shore, we crawled out into the thick mud. I scanned the area in front of us. All I saw was a grove of trees. There was nothing that looked like a cave.

"We can't just stay here looking around," Luna said. "We have to move on."

I could see the tiger splashing in the river, getting dangerously near the bank.

Suddenly, something caught my eye—it was running through the trees ahead of us. It went by too fast for me to see what it was. All I could see was that it was hairy and running on two feet.

"Do you think it's a gorilla?" Luna asked.

"Too small," I answered.

"A chimpanzee?"

I shook my head. "Too big."

"Well, I say we follow it," she said. "Maybe it knows something we don't know."

We took off after the creature.

Somewhere in the grove of trees, we lost sight of it. We kept going anyway. On the other side of the grove, we hit a wall of rocks with giant boulders in front. There was no sign of the creature. I examined the rocks quickly.

"Over there," I said, pointing to a narrow, low opening between two boulders. "Maybe that's the mouth of a cave."

We ran to the opening. It was really small. Luna dropped to the ground. Crawling on her hands and knees, she squeezed her head and shoulders through the boulders into the tight space.

"It is a cave," she called out, her legs disappearing from my sight. "Follow me inside, Tiger."

"I can't fit through there. No way."

"Neither can the tiger," she said. "You have to try."

I turned around to check on the tiger. He was no more than ten feet away. He was crouched on his hind legs, his claws extended all the way out. I knew that gesture. It's what cats do when they're about to pounce on a mouse. The tiger was getting ready to attack.

With my heart beating fast, I dove for the

opening of the cave. My head went in fine, and I was even able to wedge my shoulders through. But my middle got stuck. I sucked in my stomach, wishing I hadn't had that tuna melt for lunch. I kicked my feet and pushed against the ground, but my body wasn't going anywhere. I thought I felt the tiger's hot breath on my legs.

"Pull my arms," I called to Luna.

"I'm trying," she said. "I'm just not strong enough."

Suddenly, I felt another pair of hands grab me, pulling with such force I thought my arms might just pop out of their sockets.

One pull.

Two pulls.

On the third pull, my middle scraped through the opening. In one smooth motion, the rest of my body followed.

I was inside the cave, looking into the eyes of the hairy creature.

CHAPTER 7

It wasn't a creature. It was a human, a teenage boy kneeling on the ground next to Luna. He was very skinny, with brown curly hair that was so long, it shot out in every direction. He was dirty from head to toe. His shirt and pants were so ripped up, I could barely tell that he was wearing clothes. He had patched up the holes with leaves and mud and animal fur.

"Who are you?" I demanded.

"Well, that's not very friendly," he answered. "You might say thank you. If it weren't for me, you'd be that tiger's dinner right about now."

"Thank you for saving Tiger's life," Luna said to him.

"Tiger?" He laughed. "What kind of a name is that?"

"My real name is Tyler," I explained, although I didn't much like him laughing at my name. "Tiger's a nickname."

"I have a nickname, too. My parents used to call me D.D. It's my initials."

Luna and I exchanged shocked looks.

"D.D.?" she said slowly. "As in . . . David Dots?"

Now it was the boy's turn to look shocked.

"How do you know my name?" he asked.

"Your mother told us."

"My *mother*! How do you know her?"

"We live right next door to her in Los Angeles," I said.

"Impossible," David answered. "There's no house next door to her. Just empty lots on both sides."

"I've lived in my house since I was born," Luna said. "So it's been there for at least ten years, I can tell you that."

David looked confused, but I was beginning to understand what was going on.

"I think a lot has changed in the fifty years since you disappeared," I told him. "Your mother says that's how long you've been gone."

David got a faraway look in his eyes.

"I remember the day," he said. "My mother was making me practice the piano. I always wanted to play drums, but she insisted I learn piano. I remember the piano was next to that new frame my parents had just brought home."

"Yes," I said. "The fantastic frame. With the rabbits and owls and grapes."

"And don't forget that weird gold clock with the birds."

"You mean the broken clock with the birds?" I asked. "Not to brag or anything, but I fixed it."

"It worked fine back then," David said. "I remember it was exactly four o'clock when all the crazy stuff happened with the painting."

"Wow," Luna said. "You have a great

memory to remember the exact time."

"You don't forget a thing like that," David told her. "It's not every day you get swallowed by a painting."

The moment David said those words, it hit me. *The hour of power.* Could the frame's hour of power be from four o'clock until five o'clock? That would make sense. Maybe that's why the clock started at four and the hands stopped at five. Of course! That was the magical hour, the hour of power!

My mind was racing. But David's was still way back in the past.

"The next thing I knew," he was telling Luna, "I was being tossed around in a storm. Then I flew through the window of some ancient castle. I must have passed out after that, because I had a dream about a fat orange pig wearing a bow tie."

I had a feeling Chives wouldn't like being called fat. After all, pigs are supposed to be pudgy.

"You got sucked into your mother's painting," Luna explained to David. "She's been looking for you ever since, doing one painting after another. We saw them. There was one of yellow haystacks."

David smiled, like he was remembering a happy memory from a long time ago.

"Yes, I was there," he said. "Golden haystacks in the French countryside. I stayed there from morning to sunset. It was so peaceful."

"And there was another painting of a navy-blue sky with wild-looking swirling stars," I said.

"I was there, too," he remembered. "It was a field of dark twisted trees and the moon was such a bright yellow."

He got up and started to pace around the cave.

"I've been to hundreds of places since then," he said. "Italian villages, castles in Spain, a desert filled with melting clocks. Don't tell my mother, but I've even spent some time with a lady who hardly had any clothes on."

"The one in the clamshell," I said. "We saw."

"But if I've been gone for fifty years, living in paintings, why haven't I gotten any older?" he wondered out loud.

"Viola says that people in paintings don't change," Luna said. "She says art is ageless."

David pushed his wild hair back from his forehead. I could see that this was a lot for him to think about. At last he said, "This means that you two are from the future."

"Yup," I said. "We live in the twenty-first century. Maybe you can come back with us . . . That is, if we ever get back."

David looked at me suspiciously.

"What if you've come here to trick me?" he asked. "Do you have any proof that what you're saying is true?"

I didn't blame him for doubting us. It's not every day that two kids fly through a painting into a jungle.

"We can tell you all about the world we live in," Luna said. "It has computers and mobile phones and electric cars and 3-D movies. I saw this really scary one last week about a three-eyed monster—"

"Luna," I interrupted. "I think he gets the point."

"Those things aren't proof," David said. "You could have read about that stuff in science fiction stories."

Then it occurred to me. I did have proof. Right there in my soggy pocket. I reached in, pulled out my helicopter, and set it on the floor of the cave.

"That doesn't look like any helicopter I've ever seen," David said.

"It's an Apache Longbow," Luna told him. "That thing on the top, by the rotors, is a radar pod."

Wow, that was a surprise. Girls who collect bird feathers don't usually know much about helicopter radar technology.

"How do you know that?" I asked Luna.

"My dad's in the army," she explained. "He's a helicopter pilot overseas."

David had moved closer and was inspecting the helicopter.

"Watch this," I told him. "I bet you never had remote control radio transmitters for your toys."

I took the remote out of my pocket. It had gotten pretty soggy in the river, so I hoped it still worked. I pushed up on the throttle. The blades started to twirl; slowly at first, then they sped up. The helicopter lifted off. I moved it forward and back, up and down, and in a complete circle. Then I let it hover right in front of David.

I could see the amazement on his face.

The whirring sound of the rotors echoed loudly throughout the cave.

"Uh-oh, Tiger, look behind you," Luna whispered. "I don't think our striped friend likes the noise."

I heard a growl and turned around to face the mouth of the cave. The small opening was filled with the tiger's paw. He was digging at the ground, trying to get a grip underneath the boulder.

Tigers are strong. But are they strong enough to shove large rocks aside to get to their prey?

I didn't know the answer. All I knew was that we were trapped inside that cave with a hungry tiger trying to get in. It was no longer a safe place for us.

CHAPTER 8

"We have to get out of here," I told Luna and David.

"I've been running from that tiger for a while now," David said. "He doesn't give up easily."

"How have you escaped him?" I asked.

"All kinds of ways. Once, I climbed a tree that was so high, the branches at the top couldn't hold him. He gave up and climbed down. Another time, I hid in a troop of wild monkeys. Once, an eagle swooped down and distracted him. He chased the eagle, and I ran in the other direction."

"That was lucky," Luna said. "But we can't count on a bird showing up just when we need one."

"We can hatch our own bird," I said.

"How exactly do we do that?" David asked. "Unless you're sitting on an egg you haven't told us about."

"Luna, give me your hat," I said.

"I think I know where you're going with this," she said with a little smile.

She took off her hat and handed it to me. The feathers were wet and muddy from the river, but that worked well for my plan. I put the helicopter in front of me and wrapped the hat around it.

"Does that look anything like a bird?" I asked.

"It will when I'm finished with it," Luna said.

She arranged the feathers carefully, bunching some of them to look like wings. Others, she shaped into a tail. Then she took a brown clip out of her hair and snapped it on the front.

"It can't be a bird if it doesn't have a beak," she said.

"I hope this thing isn't too heavy to fly," I said.

I picked up the remote and pressed the throttle. The whirring started up, and slowly the helicopter rose into the air.

"We have liftoff!" I cried.

The feathery thing circled the cave. It wasn't the most real-looking bird I'd ever seen. But it wasn't bad, either.

"Do you think this will trick the tiger?" Luna asked me.

"We have a shot. Maybe to tiger eyes, this will look like a delicious turkey dinner."

The sound of the whirring had excited the tiger again. His paw clawed even faster at the ground. The boulder wiggled a bit. He was making progress.

"So here's the big question," Luna said. "How do we get out of the cave and launch this thing without the tiger snatching us?"

We were quiet. That was a tough question. Then David got up and took the controller from my hand.

"You mind if I try operating this?" he asked. "It looks like fun."

"This isn't really the best time to be playing with toys," I told him. But by that time, he already had his hands on the throttle. The birdlike helicopter zoomed wildly in the air. It looked like it was going to crash into the cave wall.

"You have to control it," I said. "Press the throttle to the left. Now right. Now down. Good, go easy. Just hover two or three feet off the ground."

"I'm getting it," David said.

"That's good. Now maybe you should stop playing with it. We have to figure out how to get out of here."

"I already have," David said. "Here's the plan. I'll go out first. I'll hover the helicopter

right in front of the tiger's nose. Then *whoosh* . . . I'll send it flying in the air. With any luck, he'll take off after it. You guys can sneak out and run in the opposite direction, back to the river."

"What about you?" I asked.

"Don't worry about me," he said. "I know my way around this jungle. I'll meet up with you."

"Maybe we should wait until it's dark out," Luna suggested.

"We can't," I said, looking at my Batman watch. "It's almost five o'clock."

"So? What happens then?"

"Well, if my theory is right, that's when the magic hour ends. The hour of power."

"Tiger, what are you talking about?" Luna asked.

"Remember when Viola talked about how

the frame had an hour of power? I think it's from four to five o'clock. That's why the frame's powers got active when I set the clock to four. And I bet at five, they're over."

"Hmmmm." Luna rubbed her chin like she was thinking hard. "And after that, whoever is left inside the painting stays inside."

"That's what I think."

"That would explain what happened to me," David said. "I was tossing about for hours in that storm. When I finally woke up in the grand hall of the castle with all those strange paintings around me, it was way past five."

"But if we're back at the very spot where we landed . . . at five o'clock . . . then maybe we'll be able to go back into the painting and return home," I said. "It's our only hope, anyway."

"Do you know what this means, David?" Luna said. "If Tiger's theory is right, you can come home with us."

Luna broke into a big smile and threw her arms around him. That was a brave thing to do, considering he hadn't taken a bath in fifty years.

"Let's just get out of this cave first," was all he said.

I pointed to my watch. It was nearing five o'clock.

"We don't have long. We have to move fast. David, are you ready?"

"Let's fly this thing," he said.

He took the helicopter and placed it at the mouth of the cave. The tiger had removed his paw, but I could hear him sniffing at the entrance. He smelled human flesh.

"Good luck, everyone," David said.

He stuck his head out of the opening. Then, quick as a cheetah, he squirmed out of the cave. As soon as he was out, I heard the whirring of the helicopter.

"We have liftoff!" David yelled.

I crept over to the opening and peeked outside. I saw the helicopter hovering in midair a few feet from the cave entrance. The tiger was tracking it with his eyes. David was behind one of the boulders, his hand clutching the controller.

"Okay, boy," David whispered. "Let's see what you've got."

He pushed his thumb on the throttle, and the helicopter zoomed through the air. The tiger followed it with his glowing yellow eyes. All at once, he sprang to his feet. Turning his powerful body in the direction of the helicopter, he took off running.

The chase was on.

CHAPTER 9

Luna poked her head outside the cave. "I can't see them," she whispered. "It's all clear."

She crawled out of the opening and reached back in to help me out.

"Think *skinny* and get out here," she said.

I wished I were as thin as David, but then, he probably wished he'd had a tuna melt for lunch. I tried going out feetfirst this time, and it worked better. I wiggled and squirmed my way out of the cave, with only a little help from Luna.

The rain had stopped. Some sun filtered through the trees. I looked around for signs of David or the tiger. There weren't any.

"Look," Luna said. "Over there."

Two sets of footprints led off into the jungle. One set was human, the other was tiger. They were headed in the opposite direction of the river.

"Now is our chance," I said. "Let's go. We only have a few minutes."

"I can run like the wind," Luna said. She took off into the grove of trees. We sprinted across the soggy jungle floor and soon we were at the river. We jumped in and swam fast, all the way to the other side.

"Now where?" Luna asked as we pulled

ourselves onto the shore.

"We have to head back to the exact spot where we landed," I said. "Can you get us there?"

"Yes," she said. "I remember what it looked like in the painting. Tall grass, a big blue-green tree surrounded by a clump of red jungle flowers. And a tiger crouched near the tree."

"I was hoping you wouldn't remember that part," I said. "I'm not happy about seeing him again."

We took off running across the jungle floor. The rain started up, coming down in heavy silver streaks. Soon, we passed the thicket of tall grass where we had stopped to rest.

"There are the red flowers," Luna said,

pointing to a clearing up ahead.

"And that's the tree where the tiger was crouching when we landed."

We bolted for the spot.

When we reached it, I checked my watch. It was two minutes to five.

"Okay, we're here. Now what?" Luna asked.

"Now we wait until five o'clock. Then we see what happens."

"We have to find David," Luna said.

I put my hands up to my mouth and called out.

"David! David! We're over here. Come here, and hurry!"

There was no answer.

"David!" I called again.

I heard a whirring sound nearby. I looked up and saw the helicopter, hovering next to the big dark tree where we stood. But where was David?

Then I saw him. Still clutching the controller in one hand, he was starting to climb up the trunk of the tree. The tiger was approaching the tree, growling at the feathery helicopter.

"David! You can't go up there!" Luna called. "You have to come with us."

"I'm going to the top," he called back. "The tiger knows not to follow me there. I'll be safe."

"But you'll be out of the picture!" I called to him. "There's no top of the tree in the painting."

"Yes, but there is a tiger in the painting," he called. "And he's ready to pounce, just like this one. If we copy the painting exactly, that will get you home."

"But, David!" Luna called. "What's going to happen to you?"

"So long, you two," he shouted. "Maybe someday we'll meet again and I'll return your helicopter."

I heard a low growl. I turned to see the tiger's attention had switched from the fake bird to us. He was standing directly under the tree. Crouched down on all fours, his eyes glowed and his jaw hung open, showing his sharp teeth. He sniffed the air, ready to attack. It was just like in the painting. He took a step toward us.

"Oh no!" Luna screamed.

Just then, the hand on my Batman watch moved. Big hand on the twelve, little hand on the five.

"It's the hour of power!" I yelled.

"The hour of power!" Luna joined in.

"The hour of power," we heard David say from the treetop.

Our voices echoed throughout the jungle. The tiger froze in midstep. The world seemed to stop.

Before we knew it, the jungle disappeared and we were tumbling back into darkness.

CHAPTER 10

All I remember seeing were the stairs, thousands of them. I don't know if we were climbing them or flying over them. We tumbled head over heels through the darkness. I had the feeling we were moving at the speed of light.

"Tiger!" I heard Luna's voice echo all around me.

"I'm here," I called back to her.

As we somersaulted through space, the

sound of the rain and thunder grew dimmer and dimmer. The sound of ripping grew louder. Then I saw the hole in the painting. Was that a face at the other end of it? I squinted.

Yes, it was. The face of an orange pig.

In one tremendous burst of speed, we shot out of the painting into Viola Dots's living room. We knocked poor Chives to the ground. Immediately, I spun around to look at the painting, just in time to see the hole close up completely. The sound of wind and thunder stopped. The air became still. The painting looked like it always had. It was as if nothing had happened.

"Oh my! Oh my!" Viola Dots was screaming. "We thought we'd never see you again."

Luna climbed off Chives and started to

talk, in great gushes of words.

"We were there," she said. "In the jungle painting. And we saw David. He's been all over. He lives in whatever painting is in the frame. His hair is really messy and he loves helicopters. He's there right now, in the jungle."

"You saw him?" Viola said. "But why didn't he return with you?"

"He stayed back to save our lives," Luna said. "If he hadn't, we would have been attacked by that tiger. He's a hero! Your son is a hero, Mrs. Dots."

"But if he's still there, then he's in danger," she said. "That tiger . . . those jaws . . ."

She was right!

"Come with me, Chives," I said. "We

have to replace that painting!"

I hurried over to the wall. Quickly, I flipped through several of Viola's paintings.

"There," I said. "This is a good one."

It was a painting of old-fashioned men and women, all dressed up. Some were carrying umbrellas. They were strolling in a park by the side of a peaceful river. Beautiful boats sailed by. Everyone looked like they were having a wonderful time.

Chives and I carried the painting over to the frame. We lifted out the tiger painting and replaced it with the peaceful scene by the river.

"David should be safe there," I told Mrs. Dots.

"Ah, yes," Chives said. "Paris is lovely in fine weather."

"Nonsense," Viola cried. "We can't leave poor David there. He belongs at home, with me. You must go back and get him immediately."

I looked at my watch. It was five minutes after five. The hour of power was over.

"We can't," I told her.

"I would go myself," she said, "but I'm too old. I'd never survive the journey."

"I would be pleased to go, Madame," Chives said.

"Don't be ridiculous, Chives," she snapped. "You're a pig. Do you see any pigs in that painting?"

Chives looked a little hurt. Luna went to him and patted him on his chubby belly.

"You're a very handsome pig," she said. "The best-dressed pig I've ever met."

That seemed to make him happy.

"The hour of power is over for today," I explained to Mrs. Dots. "If my theory is right, I think it only lasts from four to five o'clock."

"Fine. Then come back tomorrow at four," she said. "And you'll bring my son back to me."

"We're having a family picnic in the park tomorrow at four," Luna said. "I can't come then."

"And I have a soccer game," I said. "I can't miss it. I'm my team's secret weapon."

To be honest, I'm not my team's secret weapon. In fact, on a very good day, I'm a below-average soccer player. And another thing: I didn't know what time my soccer game was. I just wanted some time to think things over before I went zooming back into another painting. Luna and I were lucky that we had escaped the jungle this time. Another day, we might not be so lucky. But Viola Dots is not the kind of woman who likes to hear the word *no*.

"When will you come back?" she said. "Monday? Tuesday? Wednesday?"

I didn't answer.

"Honestly, am I going to have to name every day of the week?" she said.

Luna went up to Viola.

"I will help you find David," she said. "But the first thing I'm going to do is give you a big hug. My grandma says that a hug is the best medicine for whatever is hurting you."

Luna put her arms around Viola's waist.

"Come on, Tiger," she said. "You too."

I wasn't exactly thrilled about the idea, so I kind of threw one arm around her and one around Luna. Just for a second, though.

I thought Viola Dots was going to faint right then and there. I have never seen anyone look so surprised. Chives grinned and let out a squeaky little pig giggle that didn't go with his top hat and tie.

When we all let go of one another. Viola straightened her headband and her necklace.

"Then it's settled," she said.

"Are you in, Tiger?" Luna asked me.

I wasn't about to let Luna Lopez be braver than me.

"I'm in if you're in," I answered.

"I'll wait to hear from both of you," Viola said. "Just make it soon. Oh, and tell no one. Until David is found, no one must know. I won't have the whole neighborhood chattering about this."

As we left the house, I could hear Viola asking Chives for a cup of tea.

"Not too full," she barked. "And not too hot, but not too cold, either. Two sugars. And I'll need some more green paint. Not too dark, but not too light, either."

We headed back to our duplex just as my mom and Maggie were pulling up in the driveway.

"I see you and Luna have become friends," my mom said. "Did you kids do something exciting this afternoon?"

"We just hung out," I said. "Turns out there's a lot of interesting things to see right here in our neighborhood."

I could see Luna stifle a giggle.

Maggie climbed out of the car. Her face was covered in chocolate frosting.

Obviously she hadn't understood that the Elmo cakes weren't for her.

"Did you see any orange pigs?" she asked.

"Just one," I answered. "He says hi."

"Goody," she said. "I'm going to go draw a picture of him."

The little frosting face skipped happily down the driveway and into the house.

"That's nice of you, Tiger," my mom said. "It's good to encourage a child's imagination."

Wow, Mom, I thought. *If only you could imagine what I've seen. If only you could know that Luna and I traveled over time and space into the world of art.*

No. There's no way anyone could imagine that.

But I'm here to tell you. It actually happened. And I had a feeling it was going to happen again very soon.

ABOUT THE
PAINTING

Surprised! or *Tiger in a Tropical Storm* by Henri Rousseau

Henri Rousseau, *Surprised!* © The National Gallery, London. Bought, with the aid of a
substantial donation from the Hon. Walter H. Annenberg, 1972

Surprised!, sometimes called *Tiger in a Tropical Storm*, is a real work of art, painted in 1891 by the French artist Henri Rousseau. It shows a tiger, lit up by a bolt of lightning, about to attack its prey in the midst of a raging storm. It was created with oil paints on canvas. Rousseau used many layers of paint and many shades of green to capture the colorful feel of the jungle. He used strands of silver paint scattered diagonally across the canvas to depict the windblown rain. Notice in the painting that we never see what the tiger is hunting. Its prey is beyond the edge of the canvas so we are left to wonder what the result of the hunt might be.

Henri Rousseau was born on May 21, 1844, in Laval, France. As a young man, he worked for a lawyer and then served in the army. When he moved to Paris, he became a tax collector at the entrance to the city. He worked at that job until he was almost fifty. Only then did he become a full-time artist.

Rousseau is known as a self-taught painter, which means he never formally studied art. During his lifetime, his work was not accepted by the official art world in Paris. In fact, when he first showed *Surprised!* in 1891, it was made fun of by art reviewers. Many critics thought his work was childish.

Rousseau is best known for his paintings that show humans or wild animals in jungle-like settings. *Surprised!* is the first of his jungle paintings. These paintings often have a dreamy quality. They are not representations of an actual jungle. Rousseau never saw a real jungle. In fact, he never even left France. Instead, he studied plants and animals at the botanical gardens in Paris, and learned to draw wild animals from books and magazines. Perhaps that is why his paintings do not seem realistic.

Later in his life, Rousseau's work was discovered by a new generation of young artists who liked the strong emotions his paintings showed. When Rousseau died in 1910, he had made very little money from his art. Yet his paintings went on to influence a generation of famous artists, including the great Pablo Picasso. Today, they are among the most well-known paintings in the world of art.

Surprised! hangs in the National Gallery in London, England.

ABOUT THE AUTHOR

Lin Oliver is the *New York Times* best-selling author of more than thirty books for young readers. She is also a film and television producer, having created shows for Nickelodeon, PBS, Disney Channel, and Fox. The cofounder and executive director of the Society of Children's Book Writers and Illustrators, she loves to hang out with children's book creators. Lin lives in Los Angeles, in the shadow of the Hollywood sign, but when she travels, she visits the great paintings of the world and imagines what it would be like to be inside the painting—so you might say she carries her own Fantastic Frame with her!

ABOUT THE ILLUSTRATOR

Samantha Kallis is a Los Angeles–based illustrator and visual development artist. Since graduating from Art Center College of Design in Pasadena, California, in 2010, her work has been featured in television, film, publishing, and galleries throughout the world. Samantha can be found most days on the porch of her periwinkle-blue Victorian cottage, where she lives with her husband and their two cats. More of her work can be seen on her website: www.samkallis.com.